A Report for

CH00864684

(Franz Kafka)
Transl. Ian Johnston

KARTINDO PUBLISHING HOUSE (Kartindo.com)

Esteemed Gentlemen of the Academy!

You show me the honour of calling upon me to submit a report to the Academy concerning my previous life as an ape.

In this sense, unfortunately, I cannot comply with your request. Almost five years separate me from my existence as an ape, a short time perhaps when measured by the calendar, but endlessly long to gallop through, as I have done, at times accompanied by splendid men, advice, applause, and orchestral music, but basically alone, since all those accompanying me held themselves back a long way from the barrier, in order to preserve the image. This achievement would have been impossible if I had stubbornly wished to hold onto my origin, onto the memories of my youth.

Giving up that obstinacy was, in fact, the highest command that I gave myself. I, a free ape, submitted myself

KARTINDO PUBLISHING HOUSE (Kartindo.com)

to this yoke. In so doing, however, my memories for their part constantly closed themselves off against me. If people had wanted it, my journey back at first would have been possible through the entire gateway which heaven builds over the earth, but as my development was whipped onwards, the gate simultaneously grew lower and narrower all the time. I felt myself more comfortable and more enclosed in the world of human beings. The storm which blew me out of my past eased off. Today it is only a gentle breeze which cools my heels. And the distant hole through which it comes and through which I once came has become so small that, even if I had sufficient power and will to run back there, I would have to scrape the fur off my body in order to get through. Speaking frankly, as much as I like choosing metaphors for these things—speaking frankly: your experience as apes,

KARTINDO PUBLISHING HOUSE (Kartindo.com)

gentlemen—to the extent that you have something of that sort behind you—cannot be more distant from you than mine is from me. But it tickles at the heels of everyone who walks here on earth, the small chimpanzee as well as the great Achilles.

In the narrowest sense, however, I can perhaps answer your question, nonetheless, and indeed I do so with great pleasure.

The first thing I learned was to give a handshake. The handshake displays candour. Today, when I stand at the highpoint of my career, may I add to that first handshake also my candid words. For the Academy it will not provide anything essentially new and will fall far short of what people have asked of me and what with the best will I cannot speak about—but nonetheless it should demonstrate the line by which someone who was an ape was forced into the world of men and which he has continued there. Yet I would certainly not permit myself to say even the trivial things which follow if I were not completely sure of myself and if my position on all the great music hall stages of the civilized world had not established itself unassailably.

I come from the Gold Coast. For an account of how I was captured I rely on the reports of strangers. A hunting expedition from the firm of Hagenback—incidentally, since then I have already emptied a number of bottles of good red wine with the leader of that expedition—lay hidden in the bushes by the shore when I ran down in the evening in the middle of a band of apes for a drink. Someone fired a shot. I was the only one struck. I received two hits.

One was in the cheek—that was superficial. But it left behind a large hairless red scar which earned me the name Red Peter—a revolting name, completely inappropriate, presumably something invented by an ape, as if the only difference between me and the recently deceased trained ape Peter, who was well known here and there, was the red patch on my cheek. But this is only by the way.

The second shot hit me below the hip. It was serious. It's the reason that today I still limp a little. Recently I read in an article by one of the ten thousand gossipers who vent their opinions about me in the newspapers that my ape nature is not yet entirely repressed. The proof is that when visitors come I take pleasure in pulling off my trousers to show the entry wound caused by this shot. That fellow should have each finger of his writing hand shot off one by one. So far as I am concerned, I may pull my trousers down in front of anyone I like. People will not find there anything other than well cared for fur and the scar from—let us select here a

KARTINDO PUBLISHING HOUSE (Kartindo.com)

precise word for a precise purpose, something that will not be misunderstood—the scar from a wicked shot. Everything is perfectly open; there is nothing to hide. When it comes to a question of the truth, every great mind discards the most subtle refinements of manners. However, if that writer were to pull down his trousers when he gets a visitor, that would certainly produce a different sight, and I'll take it as a sign of reason that he does not do that. But then he should not bother me with his delicate sensibilities.

After those shots I woke up—and here my own memory gradually begins—in a cage between decks on the Hagenbeck steamship. It was no four-sided cage with bars, but only three walls fixed to a crate, so that the crate constituted the fourth wall. The whole thing was too low to stand upright and too narrow for sitting down. So I crouched with bent knees, which shook all the time, and since at first I probably did not wish to see anyone and to remain constantly in the darkness, I turned towards the crate, while the bars of the cage cut into the flesh on my back. People consider such confinement of wild animals beneficial in the very first period of time, and today I cannot deny, on the basis of my own experience, that in a human sense that is, in fact, the case.

But at that time I didn't think about it. For the first time in my life I was without a way out—at least there was no direct way out. Right in front of me was the crate, its boards fitted closely together. Well, there was a hole running right through the boards. When I first discovered it, I welcomed it with a blissfully happy howl of ignorance. But this hole was not nearly big enough to stick my tail through, and all the power of an ape could not make it any bigger.

According to what I was told later, I am supposed to have made remarkably little noise. From that people concluded that either I must soon die or, if I succeeded in surviving the first critical period, I would be very capable of being trained. I survived this period. Muffled sobbing, painfully searching out fleas, wearily licking a coconut, banging my skull against the wall of the crate, sticking out my tongue when anyone came near—these were the first occupations in my new life. In all of them, however, there was only one feeling: no way out. Nowadays, of course, I can portray those ape-like feelings only with human words and, as a result, I misrepresent them. But even if I can no longer attain the old truth of the ape, at least it lies in the direction I have described—of that there is no doubt.

KARTINDO PUBLISHING HOUSE (Kartindo.com)

Up until then I had had so many ways out, and now I no longer had one. I was tied down. If they had nailed me down, my freedom to move would not have been any less. And why? If you scratch raw the flesh between your toes, you won't find the reason. If you press your back against the bars of the cage until it almost slices you in two, you won't find the answer. I had no way out, but I had to come up with one for myself. For without that I could not live. Always in front of that crate wall—I would inevitably have died a miserable death. But according to Hagenbeck, apes belong at the crate wall—well, that meant I had to cease being an ape. A clear and beautiful train of thought, which I must have planned somehow with my belly, since apes think with their bellies.

I'm worried that people do not understand precisely what I mean by a way out. I use the word in its most common and fullest sense. I am deliberately not saying freedom. I do not mean this great feeling of freedom on all sides. As an ape, I perhaps recognized it, and I have met human beings who yearn for it. But as far as I am concerned, I did not demand freedom either then or today. Incidentally, among human beings people all too often are deceived by freedom. And since freedom is reckoned among the most sublime feelings, the corresponding disappointment is also among the most sublime. In the variety shows, before my entrance, I have often watched a pair of artists busy on trapezes high up in the roof. They swung themselves, they rocked back and forth, they jumped, they hung in each other's arms, one held the other by clenching the hair with his teeth. "That, too, is human freedom," I thought, "self-controlled movement." What a mockery of sacred nature! At such a sight, no structure would stand up to the laughter of the apes.

No, I didn't want freedom. Only a way out—to the right or left or anywhere at all. I made no other demands, even if the way out should be only an illusion. The demand was small; the disappointment would not be any greater—to move on further, to move on further! Only not to stand still with arms raised, pressed again a crate wall.

Today I see clearly that without the greatest inner calm I would never have been able to get out. And in fact I probably owe everything that I have become to the calmness which came over me after the first days there on the ship. And, in turn, I owe that calmness to the people on the ship.

They are good people, in spite of everything. Today I still enjoy remembering the clang of their heavy steps, which used to echo then in my half sleep. They had the habit of tackling everything extremely slowly. If one of them wanted to rub his eyes, he raised his hand as if it were a hanging weight. Their jokes were gross but hearty. Their laughter was always mixed with a rasp which sounded dangerous but meant nothing. They always had something in their mouths to spit out, and they didn't care where they spat. They always complained that my fleas sprung over onto them, but they were never seriously angry at me because of it. They even knew that fleas liked being in my fur and that fleas are jumpers. They learned to live with that. When they had no duties, sometimes a few of them sat down in a semi-circle around me. They didn't speak much, but only made noises to each other and smoked their pipes, stretched out on the crates. They slapped their knees as soon as I made the slightest movement, and from time to time one of them would pick up a stick and tickle me where I liked it. If I were invited today to make a journey on that ship, I'd certainly decline the invitation, but it's equally certain that the memories I could dwell on of the time there between the decks would not be totally hateful.

The calmness which I acquired in this circle of people prevented me above all from any attempt to escape. Looking at it nowadays, it seems to me as if I had at least sensed that I had to find a way out if I wanted to live, but that this way out could not be reached by escaping. I no longer know if escape was possible, but I think it was: for an ape it should always be possible to flee. With my present teeth I have to be careful even with the ordinary task of cracking a nut, but then I must have been able, over time, to succeed in chewing through the lock on the door. I didn't do that. What would I have achieved by doing that?

No sooner would I have stuck my head out, than they would have captured me again and locked me up in an even worse cage. Or I could have taken refuge unnoticed among the other animals—say, the boa constrictors opposite me—and breathed my last in their embraces. Or I could have managed to steal way up to the deck and jumped overboard. Then I'd have tossed back and forth for a while on the ocean and drowned. Acts of despair. I did not think things through in such a human way, but under the influence of my surroundings conducted myself as if I had worked things out.

I did not work things out, but I observed well in complete tranquility. I saw these men going back and forth, always the same faces, the same movements. Often it seemed to me as if there was only one man. So the man or these men went undisturbed. A lofty purpose dawned on me. No one

KARTINDO PUBLISHING HOUSE (Kartindo.com)

promised me that if I could become like them the cage would be removed. Such promises, apparently impossible to fulfill, were not made. But if one makes the fulfillment good, then later the promises appear precisely there where one had looked for them earlier without success. Now, these men in themselves were nothing which attracted me very much. If I had been a follower of that freedom I just mentioned, I would certainly have preferred the ocean to the way out displayed in the dull gaze of these men. But in any case, I observed them for a long time before I even thought about such things—in fact, the accumulated observations first pushed me in the proper direction.

It was so easy to imitate these people. I could already spit on the first day. We used to spit in each other's faces. The only difference was that I licked my face clean afterwards. They did not. Soon I was smoking a pipe, like an old man, and if I then pressed my thumb down into the bowl of the pipe, the entire area between decks cheered. Still, for a long time I did not understand the difference between an empty and a full pipe.

I had the greatest difficulty with the bottle of alcohol. The smell was torture to me. I forced myself with all my power, but weeks went by before I could overcome my reaction. Curiously enough, the people took this inner struggle more seriously than anything else about me. In my memories I don't distinguish the people, but there was one who always came back, alone or with comrades, day and night, at different times. He'd stand with a bottle in front of me and give me instructions. He did not understand me. He wanted to solve the riddle of my being. He used to uncork the bottle slowly and then look at me, in order to test if I had understood. I confess that I always looked at him with wildly over-eager attentiveness. No human teacher has ever found in the entire world such a student of human beings.

After he'd uncorked the bottle, he'd raise it to his mouth. I'd gaze at him, right at his throat. He would nod, pleased with me, and set the bottle to his lips. Delighted with my gradual understanding, I'd squeal and scratch myself all over, wherever it was convenient. He was happy. He'd set the bottle to his mouth and take a swallow. Impatient and desperate to emulate him, I would defecate over myself in my cage—and that again gave him great satisfaction. Then, holding the bottle at arm's length and bringing it up again with a swing, he'd drink it down with one gulp, exaggerating his backward bending as a way of instructing me. Exhausted with so much great effort, I could no longer follow and hung weakly onto the bars,

KARTINDO PUBLISHING HOUSE (Kartindo.com)

while he ended the theoretical lesson by rubbing his belly and grinning.

Now the practical exercises first began. Was I not already too tired out by the theoretical part? Yes, indeed, far too weary. That's part of my fate. Nonetheless, I'd grab the proffered bottle as well as I could and uncork it trembling. Once I'd managed to do that, new forces gradually take over. I lift the bottle—with hardly any difference between me and the original—put it to my lips—and throw it away in disgust, in disgust, although it is empty and filled only with the smell, throw it with disgust onto the floor. To the sorrow of my teacher, to my own greater sorrow. And I still do not console him or myself when, after throwing away the bottle, I do not forget to give my belly a splendid rub and to grin as I do so.

All too often, the lesson went that way. And to my teacher's credit, he was not angry with me. Well, sometimes he held his burning pipe against my fur in some place or other which I could reach only with difficulty, until it began to burn. But then he would put it out himself with his huge good hand. He wasn't angry with me. He realized that we were fighting on the same side against ape nature and that I had the more difficult part.

What a victory it was for him and for me, however, when one evening in front of a large circle of onlookers—perhaps it was a celebration, a gramophone was playing, and officer was wandering around among the people—when on this evening, at a moment when no one was watching, I grabbed a bottle of alcohol which had been inadvertently left standing in front of my cage, uncorked it just as I had been taught, amid the rising attention of the group, set it against my mouth and, without hesitating, with my mouth making no grimace, like an expert drinker, with my eyes rolling around, splashing the liquid in my throat, I really and truly drank the bottle empty, and then threw it away, no longer in despair, but like an artist. Well, I did forget to scratch my belly. But instead of that, because I couldn't do anything else, because I had to, because my senses were roaring, I cried out a short and good "Hello!" breaking out into human sounds. And with this cry I sprang into the community of human beings, and I felt its echo—"Just listen. He's talking!"—like a kiss on my entire sweat-soaked body.

I'll say it again: imitating human beings was not something which pleased me. I imitated them because I was looking for a way out, for no other reason. And even in that victory little was achieved. My voice immediately failed me again. It first came back months later. My distaste for the bottle of alcohol became even stronger. But at least my direction was given to me once and for all.

When I was handed over in Hamburg to my first trainer, I soon realized the two possibilities open to me: the Zoological Garden or the Music Hall. I did not hesitate. I said to myself: use all your energy to get into the Music Hall. That is the way out. The Zoological Garden is only a new barred cage. If you go there, you're lost.

And I learned, gentlemen. Alas, one learns when one has to. Once learns when one wants a way out. One learns ruthlessly. One supervises oneself with a whip and tears oneself apart at the slightest resistance. My ape nature ran off, head over heels, out of me, so that in the process my first teacher himself almost became an ape and soon had to give up training and be carried off to a mental hospital. Fortunately he was soon discharged again.

KARTINDO PUBLISHING HOUSE (Kartindo.com)

But I went through many teachers—indeed, even several teachers at once. As I became more confident of my abilities and the general public followed my progress and my future began to brighten, I took on teachers myself, let them sit down in five interconnected rooms, and studied with them all simultaneously, by constantly leaping from one room into another.

And such progress! The penetrating effects of the rays of knowledge from all sides on my awaking brain! I don't deny the fact—I was delighted with it. But I also confess that I did not overestimate it, not even then, even less today. With an effort which up to this point has never been repeated on earth, I have attained the average education of a European. That would perhaps not amount to much, but it is something insofar as it helped me out of the cage and created this special way out for me—the way out of human beings.

KARTINDO PUBLISHING HOUSE (Kartindo.com)

There is an excellent German expression: to beat one's way through the bushes. That I have done. I have beaten my way through the bushes. I had no other way, always assuming that freedom was not a choice.

If I review my development and its goal up to this point, I do not complain. I am even satisfied. With my hands in my trouser pockets, the bottle of wine on the table, I half lie and half sit in my rocking chair and gaze out the window. If I have a visitor, I welcome him as is appropriate. My impresario sits in the parlour. If I ring, he comes and listens to what I have to say. In the evening I almost always have a performance, and my success could hardly rise any higher. When I come home late from banquets, from scientific societies, or from social gatherings in someone's home, a small half-trained female chimpanzee is waiting for me, and I take my pleasure with her the way apes do. During the day I don't want to see her. For she has in her gaze the madness of a bewildered trained animal. I'm the only one who recognizes that, and I cannot bear it.

On the whole, at any rate, I have achieved what I wished to achieve. You shouldn't say it wasn't worth the effort. In any case, I don't want any man's judgment. I only want to expand knowledge. I simply report. Even to you, esteemed gentlemen of the Academy, I have only made a report.

THE END

KARTINDO PUBLISHING HOUSE (Kartindo.com)

Printed in Great Britain
by Amazon